TOMMYSAURUS REX

DOUG TENNAPEL

WITH COLOR BY KATHERINE GARNER

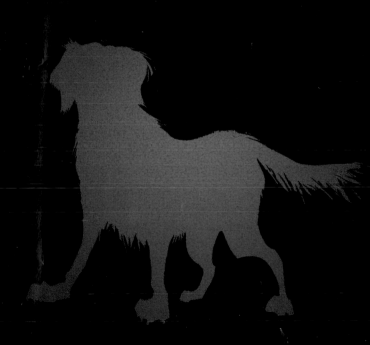

An Imprint of

I wish to thank Hugh Speed for rendering borders, Tony McVey for the cool dinosaur reference, Ray Harryhausen for the inspiration, and Philip Simon for helping me find paper. To Katherine Garner for the great color work, and to the beloved Mrs. TenNapel, you make me happy.

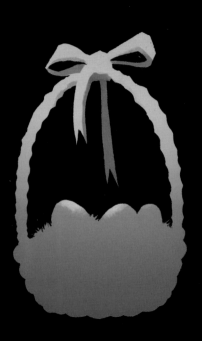

Library of Congress Control Number: 2012945113

ISBN 978-0-545-48382-7
ISBN 978-0-545-48383-4 (paperback)
10 9 8 7 6 5 4 3 2 1   13 14 15 16 17

1

GULP!
GULP!
GULP!

WILL YOU *PLEASE* COME UP FOR AIR?!

WELL, DO YOU WANT ME TO EAT 'EM OR NOT?!

WHAT'S THE BIG HURRY?

MMFFF! ...I GOTTA GO-GO-GO! ME AND TOMMY--

TOMMY AND I.

RIGHT, TOMMY AND ME ARE HAVING DOG RACES AT THE PARK. WE'RE GONNA RUN-RUN-*RUN!* BOBBY JENKINS SAYS IF WE WIN WE CAN JOIN THEIR CLUB!

3

MUNCH MUNCH MUNCH MUNCH

BAD TOMMY! GET AWAY FROM *MY* BACON!

OOF! ELY, WHY WON'T YOU TEACH GODZILLA A LITTLE *OBEDIENCE?!* THEY *CAN* BE TAUGHT, YOU KNOW!

SORRY, DAD!

I'LL TRY TO TEACH HIM SOME MANNERS AT THE PARK.

NOW I EAT *HIS* LEFT-OVERS?!

YES, DEAR.

HELLO, ELY.

GRRR

HI, MRS. COOPER.

GRRR!

RRR

STEADY... I'M RIGHT HERE WITH YOU ... NO NEED TO FREAK OUT.

YIP! YIP!

YOU NEVER DID LIKE TOMMY.

I JUST DIDN'T THINK IT WAS A GOOD IDEA TO TRY TO REPLACE A SOCIALLY CRIPPLING ABSENCE OF HUMAN FRIENDS WITH A DOG, THAT'S ALL.

REMEMBER HOW ELY WOULDN'T BELIEVE US WHEN WE SAID THE PUPPY WAS *FEMALE?*

HE SAID, "HOW CAN HE BE A *GIRL* WHEN HIS NAME IS *TOMMY?!*"

I HOPE HE'LL BE OKAY.

HOW'S IT GOING, SON?

I SHOULD HAVE HELD HIS LEASH TIGHTER! HE'D STILL BE ALIVE!

DON'T BEAT YOURSELF UP FOR THIS, SON. YOU GOTTA KEEP MOVING FORWARD.

I GUESS.

I HAVE A SURPRISE FOR YOU.

STUBBORN, NO-GOOD LLAMA...

WHAP!

HI, DAD.

YOU OKAY, MENDOZA?

I'LL BE OKAY WHEN I PUT THAT ANIMAL IN THE *GROUND* SOME GLORIOUS DAY.

PLUS SHE SMELLS EVEN WORSE THAN YOU!

NICE.

GRANDPA!

DID YOU GET ME A *PRESENT?*

I'LL BRING HIS STUFF IN.

YOU GET THE BIG ONE!

MOM NEVER LETS ME EAT A *WHOLE* STEAK!

I'LL BET YOUR MOM NEVER LETS YOU HAVE ONE OF *THESE* EITHER!

WOAAAAH!

GLUB GLUB GLUB

ROOT BEER!

24

dear Dad,
Where are you?
Where are you?
Where are you?

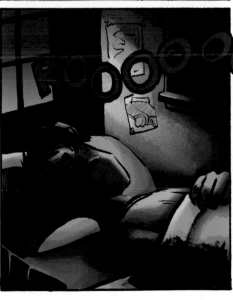

TOMMY?

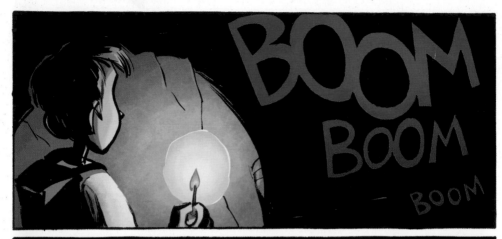

41

HERE'S A NICE STACK OF HAY FOR YOU TO SLEEP ON!

I'M SURE THAT GRAMPA WON'T MIND.

Z.

Z.

I WISH *TOMMY* COULD HAVE BEEN HERE TO MEET YOU.

OUCHEE-WAWA!

THAT'S A ...

... A T-T-T-TYRANNO-SAU-SAU-SAU ...

A T-REX.

UH-HUH! WHEEE!

I'M GOING TO NEED SOME COFFEE BEFORE I CAN HAVE MY MIND SO THOROUGHLY BLOWN.

RUMBLE RUMBLE

YOU'RE HUNGRY. LET'S FIND YOU SOMETHING TO EAT.

WAIT.

WHAT IS THAT THING GOING TO EAT?

WE'LL HAVE TO FIX THIS.

59

WHAT'S THIS ABOUT THAT T-REX TRYING TO EAT RANDY?

HUH, I WISH!

SNIFF! SNIFF!

I KNOW WHAT YOU MEAN.

ELY, MY PARK IS COVERED IN *DINOSAUR CRAP!*

I KNOW HOW THIS MUST LOOK, MAYOR. BUT LOTS OF ANIMALS GO POOP IN THE PARK.

SNIFF SNIFF

IS THAT SUPPOSED TO BE SOME SORT OF *CONSOLATION* KNOWING THAT THERE'S A POOP THE SIZE OF A BUS IN MY PARK?!

FSSSSsss

UH...

MAYOR, YOU'VE GOT TO THINK OF YOUR *VOTERS*. THEY MAY *WANT* TO SEE A REAL LIVE DINOSAUR POOP!

GOOD ONE, ELY! LET'S CHARGE MONEY WHILE WE'RE AT IT! EIGHT HUNDRED DOLLARS A PEEK!

YEAH!

PREPOSTEROUS! YOU LISTEN UP, YOUNG MAN! I DON'T WANT DINOSAUR POOP ASSOCIATED WITH MY *CAMPAIGN* OR MY *PARK!* SEE?!

SO YOU'D BETTER STOP SNOWIN' ME AND START *CLEANING UP!*

THAT'S FERTILIZER!

WAH?

SEE HOW HALF THE PARK'S GRASS HAS TURNED BROWN?

WELL, EVERYONE KNOWS THAT THE ELEMENTAL NUTRIENTS HAVE BEEN SUCKED OUT OF THE GROUND!

IS THAT RIGHT?

IT IS! WE FIGURED THAT A HEARTY LAYER OF *DINOSAUR DUNG* WOULD HELP OAKHURST PARK BE THE ENVY OF OUR NEIGHBORS!

EVEN FRESNO?

ESPECIALLY FRESNO!

THAT'S BECAUSE KING KONG IS FAKE!

IS NOT!

IS SO!

NUH-UH! I SEEN HIM! HE'S FOR *REAL*!

NO HE'S NOT! HE'S A SPECIAL EFFECT.

IF HE'S NOT REAL, THEN HOW DID THEY MAKE HIM *MOVE*?!

I DUNNO --

PERHAPS I CAN HELP EXPLAIN ...

HUH?

ACTUALLY, THEY BUILD STOP-MOTION PUPPETS OUT OF BALL-AND-SOCKET ARMATURES COVERED IN FOAM RUBBER. THEN THE ANIMATOR SUBTLY ALTERS THE MODEL'S POSITION AND SHOOTS ONE FRAME BEFORE ALTERING THE MODEL AGAIN. ACROSS A SEQUENCE OF FRAMES, INCREMENTAL CHANGES CONSTRUCT A MOVEMENT. WHEN THE FILM IS PLAYED BACK AT NORMAL SPEED, THE CHARACTER APPEARS TO MOVE OF ITS OWN VOLITION!

UH, THANKS FOR THAT... I *THINK*.

NO PROBLEM. I HEARD ABOUT THE T-REX AND THOUGHT I'D DO SOME SKETCHING.

ARE YOU GOING TO STAY UP ALL NIGHT?

I'M WRITING DAD ABOUT THE T-REX.

OH.

IF HE FINDS OUT THERE'S A DINOSAUR IN TOWN, HE'LL COME BACK FOR SURE!

WILL YOU MAIL THIS FOR ME?

YOU NEED TO GO TO BED.

PLEEEAAASE?!

RANDY   FOR DAD

87

SIT, I SAY! SIT DOWN!

HE'S DOING IT ALL WRONG.

YOU CAN DO BETTER?

COMPARED TO TEACHING A LLAMA TO SIT? TEACHING A DINOSAUR WOULD BE A PIECE O' FLAN.

STEP ASIDE. YOU HAVE TO SHOW HIM WHO IS THE BOSS.

HOW DO I DO THAT?

YOU HAVE TO GET HIS ATTENTION.

RUN FROM THE FIRE! I'M AFRAID OF FIRE! OH! I'M AFRAID!

DANG IT.

Böïnk!

?

Dad Please come and see me

SO LEMME GET THIS STRAIGHT. ELY HAS TO MAKE A T-REX DO TRICKS?

SOMETHING LIKE THAT. I'M SO NERVOUS I'M ABOUT TO JUST EXPLODE.

OH, HONEY, WE'VE ALREADY GONE OVER THIS. IT'S GOOD FOR ELY TO BE EXPOSED TO A LITTLE RESPONSIBILITY. JUST DON'T GO ALL TO TEARS AND BABY THE BOY WHEN YOU SEE HIM.

SINGLE FILE! ONE AT A TIME! THERE'S ENOUGH FOR EVERYBODY!

DAD, WHAT'S GOING ON?!

WE ALREADY PAID OFF THE NEIGHBOR'S MORTGAGE, AND NOW WE'RE WORKING ON ELY'S COLLEGE FUND!

WHAT'S WITH THE CANE? ARE YOU HURT?

OH, I'M IN EXCRUCIATING PAIN! THINGS COULDN'T BE BETTER!

101

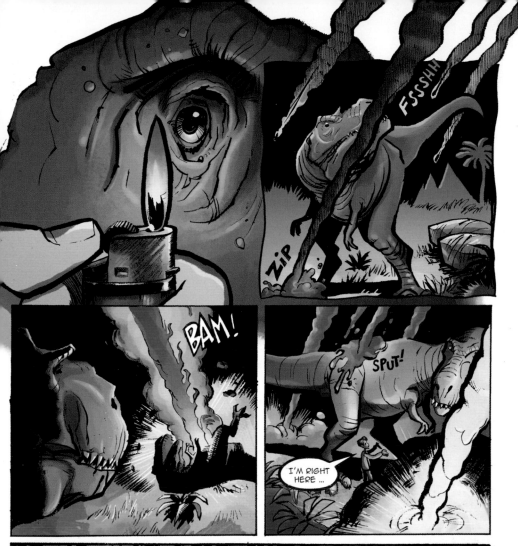

OVER HERE!

ROAR?

THAT'S RIGHT, BUDDY! IT'S ME!

SEE?

THREE CHEERS FOR TOMMY!

HIP HIP HOORAY!

HIP HIP HOORAY!

THAT'S THE FIRST TIME MY TRICK ANKLE WAS EVER WRONG!

WE WANT A PICTURE WITH THE BOY AND TOMMY!

EVERYONE GET ON THE DINO!

SCOOT IN!

THIS BRUSH IS TOO DRY! WE'VE GOTTA WORK *FAST!*

TOMMY, COME TO MY VOICE!

OVER HERE! IT'S ME, ELY!

WOAH!

COUGH COUGH

GLUNK GLUNK GLUNK

FOOM!!

WE HAVE TO LET THE FIREMEN DO THEIR JOB.

STAND BACK, KID, WE'LL PUT HIM OUT!

HELLLP!

SOMEONE'S OUT THERE!

I'M RIGHT HERE WITH YOU!

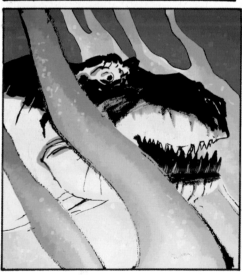

GASP!

RANDY?!

I'M FINISHED.

?

RANDY!

SOME-THING'S IN HIS MOUTH!

EVERY-BODY, GET BACK! WE GOTTA GIVE THE BOY AIR!

HE'S ALIVE! HE'S GONNA BE ALL RIGHT!

COUGH COUGH

DID YOU HEAR *THAT*?! THE BOY'S ALIVE! HE'LL BE JUST FINE!

KNOCK-KNOCK

IT'S BUCKSHOT. IS RANDY GIVING HIM TO ME?

SORRY

HE'S LETTING YOU KNOW THAT HIS APOLOGY IS SINCERE.

TOMMY'S A GIRL!

ELY?!

FORGIVEN

FORGIVEN

DOUG TENNAPEL is the creator of GHOSTOPOLIS, BAD ISLAND, and CARDBOARD. GHOSTOPOLIS was an ALA 2011 Top Ten Great Graphic Novel for Teens and a 2010 *Kirkus* Best Book of the Year. Both BAD ISLAND and CARDBOARD were *School Library Journal* Top Ten Graphic Novels in 2011 and 2012 respectively.

Doug is also the creator of the hugely popular character Earthworm Jim. He lives in Colorado Springs, Colorado, with his wife and four children.